ORORO

BEFORE THE STORM

PART 4

MARC SUMERAK	CARLO BARBERI	ANDREW PEPOY, JOHN STANISCI and M3TH	SHANE LAW@UDON
WRITER	PENCILS	INKS	COLORS

STUART IMMONEN	DAVE SHARPE	TOM VALENTE	NICOLE WILEY	CADENHEAD and PANICCIA	JOE QUESADA	DAN BUCKLEY
COVER	LETTERER	PRODUCTION	EDITOR	CONSULTING EDITORS	CHIEF	PUBLISHER

Spotlight

MARVEL
marvelkids.com

RAISED AS A THIEF ON THE STREETS OF CAIRO, EGYPT, A YOUNG ORPHAN NAMED ORORO MUNROE STRUGGLES TO SURVIVE AND TO FIND HER PLACE IN THE WORLD. UNAWARE THAT SHE WILL GROW UP TO BE **STORM--** ONE OF THE GREATEST X-MEN OF ALL TIME--YOUNG ORORO'S ADVENTURES HAVE ONLY JUST BEGUN!

visit us at www.abdopublishing.com

Reinforced library bound edition published in 2013 by Spotlight, a division of the ABDO Group, 8000 West 78th Street, Edina, Minnesota 55439. Spotlight produces high-quality reinforced library bound editions for schools and libraries. Published by agreement with Marvel Entertainment, LLC. The stories, characters, and incidents mentioned are entirely fictional. All rights reserved. Used under authorization.

Printed in the United States of America, North Mankato, Minnesota.
052012
092012
♻This book contains at least 10% recycled materials.

TM & © 2012 Marvel & Subs.

Library of Congress Cataloging-in-Publication Data

Sumerak, Marc.
  Ororo : before the Storm / story by Marc Sumerak ; art by Carlo Barberi. -- Reinforced library bound ed.
      <v. 1-> cm. -- (Ororo)
  "Marvel."
  Summary: Long before she became the X-Man known as Storm, a young orphan named Ororo Munroe stalks the streets of Cairo, stealing under the tutelage of Achmed El-Gibar and yearning for the greatness her mother knew she would find.
  ISBN 978-1-61479-024-2 (part 1) -- ISBN 978-1-61479-025-9 (part 2) -- ISBN 978-1-61479-026-6 (part 3) -- ISBN 978-1-61479-027-3 (part 4)
  1. Graphic novels. [1. Graphic novels. 2. Superheroes--Fiction. 3. Orphans--Fiction. 4. Robbers and outlaws--Fiction. 5. Cairo (Egypt)--Fiction. 6. Egypt--Fiction.] I. Barberi, Carlo, ill. II. Title.
  PZ7.7.S86Oro 2012
  741.5'973--dc23
                          2012000932
ISBN 978-1-61479-027-3 (reinforced library edition)

All Spotlight books are reinforced library binding
and manufactured in the United States of America.

So... With Barrett, um, *out* of the *picture*, what do you *think* will happen to the Opal *now*?

"I *do not know*, Hakiim..."

"...but I have a *feeling* it will *someday* find its way *back* to *where it belongs*."

"Hopefully, *we will* as well."

The Beginning...